HORRID HENRY'S
Hike

HORRiD HENRY'S
Hike

Francesca Simon
Illustrated by Tony Ross

Orion
Children's Books

Horrid Henry's Hike first appeared in *Horrid Henry
and the Mega-Mean Time Machine*
First published in Great Britain in 2005 by Orion Children's Books
Reissued in paperback in 2008 by Orion Children's Books
This edition first published
in Great Britain in 2018
by Hodder and Stoughton

1 3 5 7 9 10 8 6 4 2

A CIP catalogue record for this book
is available from the British Library.

ISBN 978 1 5101 0520 1

Printed and bound in China

The paper and board used in this book are from well-managed forests
and other responsible sources.

FSC
www.fsc.org

MIX
Paper from
responsible sources
FSC® C104740

Orion Children's Books
An imprint of
Hachette Children's Group
Part of Hodder and Stoughton
Carmelite House
50 Victoria Embankment
London EC4Y 0DZ

An Hachette UK Company
www.hachette.co.uk
www.hachettechildrens.co.uk
www.horridhenry.co.uk

To Jonathan Douglas and the
marvellous National Literacy Trust

There are many more
Horrid Henry Early Reader books available.

For a complete list visit:
www.horridhenry.co.uk

Contents

Chapter 1

Horrid Henry looked out of the
window. AAARRRGGGHHH!
It was a lovely day. The sun was
shining. The birds were tweeting.
The breeze was blowing. Little fluffy
clouds floated by in a bright blue sky.

Rats.

Why couldn't it be raining?
Or hailing?
Or sleeting?

Any minute, any second, it would happen . . . the words he'd been dreading, the words he'd give anything not to hear, the words–

"Henry! Peter! Time to go for a walk," called Mum.

"Yippee!" said Perfect Peter. "I can wear my new yellow wellies!"

"NO!" screamed Horrid Henry.

Go for a walk! Go for a walk! Didn't he walk enough already? He walked to school. He walked home from school. He walked to the TV. He walked to the computer. He walked to the sweet jar *and* all the way back to the comfy black chair.

Horrid Henry walked plenty. Ugghh.
The last thing he needed was more
walking. More chocolate, yes. More
crisps, yes. More *walking*? No way!

Why oh why couldn't his parents
ever say, "Henry! Time to play on
the computer." Or "Henry, stop
doing your homework this minute!
Time to turn on the TV."

But no. For some reason his mean, horrible parents thought he spent too much time sitting indoors. They'd been threatening for weeks to make him go on a family walk.

Now the dreadful moment had
come. His precious weekend
was ruined.

Horrid Henry hated nature.
Horrid Henry hated fresh air.

What could be more boring than walking up and down streets staring at lamp posts? Or sloshing across some stupid muddy park?

Nature smelled. Uggh! He'd much
rather be inside watching TV.

Chapter 2

Mum stomped into the sitting room. "Henry! Didn't you hear me calling?"

"No," lied Henry.

"Get your wellies on, we're going," said Dad, rubbing his hands. "What a lovely day."

"I don't want to go for a walk,"
said Henry. "I want to watch
*Rapper Zapper Zaps Terminator
Gladiator*."

"But Henry," said Perfect Peter,
"fresh air and exercise are so good
for you."

"I don't care!" shrieked Henry.

Horrid Henry stomped downstairs and flung open the front door. He breathed in deeply, hopped on one foot, then shut the door.

"There! Done it. Fresh air *and* exercise," snarled Henry.

"Henry, we're going," said Mum. "Get in the car."

Henry's ears pricked up.

"The car?" said Henry. "I thought we were going for a walk."

"We are," said Mum. "In the countryside."

"Hurray!" said Perfect Peter. "A nice *long* walk."

"NOOOO!" howled Henry. Plodding along in the boring old park was bad enough, with its mouldy leaves and dog poo and stumpy trees. But at least the park wasn't very big. But the *countryside*?

The countryside was enormous!
They'd be walking for hours, days,
weeks, months, till his legs wore
down to stumps and his feet fell
off. And the countryside was so
dangerous! Horrid Henry was sure
he'd be swallowed up by quicksand
or trampled to death by marauding
chickens.

"I live in the city!" shrieked Henry. "I don't want to go to the country!"

"Time you got out more," said Dad.

"But look at those clouds," moaned Henry, pointing to a fluffy wisp. "We'll get soaked."

"A little water never hurt anyone,"
said Mum.

Oh yeah? Wouldn't they be sorry
when he died of pneumonia.

"I'm staying here and that's final!"
screamed Henry.

"Henry, we're waiting," said Mum.

"Good," said Henry.

"*I'm* all ready, Mum," said Peter.

"I'm going to start deducting pocket money," said Dad. "5p, 10p, 15p, 20—"

Horrid Henry pulled on his wellies, stomped out of the door and got in the car. He slammed the door as hard as he could. It was so unfair!

Why did he never get to do what *he* wanted to do?

Now he would miss the first time
Rapper Zapper had ever slugged it
out with Terminator Gladiator. And
all because he had to go on a long,
boring, exhausting, horrible hike. He
was so miserable he didn't even have
the energy to kick Peter.

"Can't we just walk round the block?" moaned Henry.

"N–O spells no," said Dad. "We're going for a lovely walk in the countryside and that's that."

Chapter 3

Horrid Henry slumped miserably in his seat. Boy would they be sorry when he was gobbled up by goats.

Boo hoo, if only we hadn't gone on that walk in the wilds, Mum would wail.

Henry was right, we should have listened to him, Dad would sob. I miss Henry, Peter would howl. I'll never eat goat's cheese again. And now it's too late, they would shriek.

If only, thought Horrid Henry. That would serve them right.

All too soon, Mum pulled into a car park, on the edge of a small wood.

"Wow," said Perfect Peter. "Look at all those lovely trees."

"Bet there are werewolves hiding there," muttered Henry. "And I hope they come and eat *you!*"

"Mum!" squealed Peter. "Henry's trying to scare me."

"Don't be horrid, Henry," said Mum.

Horrid Henry looked around him.

There was a gate, leading to endless meadows bordered by hedgerows. A muddy path wound through the trees and across the fields. A church spire stuck up in the distance.

"Right, I've seen the countryside,
let's go home," said Henry.
Mum glared at him.

"What?" said Henry, scowling.

"Let's enjoy this lovely day,"
said Dad, sighing.

"So what do we do now?" said Henry.

"Walk," said Dad.

"Where?" said Henry.

"Just walk," said Mum, "and enjoy the beautiful scenery."

Henry groaned.

"We're heading for the lake," said Dad, striding off. "I've brought bread and we can feed the ducks."

"But *Rapper Zapper* starts in an hour!"

"Tough," said Mum.

Mum, Dad, and Peter headed
through the gate into the field.
Horrid Henry trailed behind them
walking as slowly as he could.

"Ahh, breathe the lovely fresh air,"
said Mum.

"We should do this more often,"
said Dad.

Henry sniffed. The horrible smell
of manure filled his nostrils.

"Ewww, smelly," said Henry. "Peter, couldn't you wait?"

"MUM!" shrieked Peter. "Henry called me smelly."

"Did not!"

"Did too!"

"Did not, smelly."

"WAAAAAAAAA!" wailed Peter. "Tell him to stop!"

"Don't be horrid, Henry!" screamed Mum. Her voice echoed. A dog walker passed her, and glared.

"Peter, would you rather run a mile, jump a stile, or eat a country pancake?" said Henry sweetly.

"Ooh," said Peter. "I love pancakes. And a country one must be even more delicious than a city one."

"Ha ha," cackled Horrid Henry, sticking out his tongue. "Fooled you. Peter wants to eat cowpats!"

"MUM!" screamed Peter.

Chapter 4

Henry walked.

And walked.

And walked.

His legs felt heavier, and heavier, and heavier.

"This field is muddy," moaned Henry.

"I'm bored," groaned Henry.

"My feet hurt," whined Henry.

"Can't we go home? We've already walked miles," whinged Henry.

"We've been walking for ten minutes," said Dad.

"Please can we go on walks more often," said Perfect Peter. "Oh, look at those fluffy little sheepies!"

Horrid Henry pounced. He was a zombie biting the head off the hapless human.

"AAAAEEEEEE!" squealed Peter.

"Henry!" screamed Mum.

"Stop it!" screamed Dad.
"Or no TV for a week."

When he was king, thought
Horrid Henry, any parent who
made their children go on a hike
would be dumped barefoot in
a scorpion-infested desert.

Plod. Plod. Plod.
Horrid Henry dragged his feet.
Maybe his horrible mean parents
would get fed up waiting for
him and turn back, he thought,
kicking some mouldy leaves.

Squelch.

Squelch.

Squelch.

Oh no, not *another*
muddy meadow.

And then suddenly Horrid Henry
had an idea.

Chapter 5

What was he thinking? All that fresh air must be rotting his brain. The sooner they got to the stupid lake, the sooner they could get home for the *Rapper Zapper Zaps Terminator Gladiator.*

"Come on, everyone, let's run!" shrieked Henry. "Race you down the hill to the lake!"

"That's the spirit, Henry," said
Dad. Horrid Henry dashed
past Dad.

"OW!" shrieked Dad, tumbling
into the stinging nettles.

Horrid Henry whizzed past Mum.

"Eww!" shrieked Mum, slipping
in a cowpat.

Splat!

Horrid Henry pushed past Peter.

"Waaa!" wailed Peter.
"My wellies are getting dirty."

Horrid Henry scampered down the
muddy path.

"Wait Henry!" yelped Mum.
"It's too slipp – aaaiiieeeee!"

Mum slid down the path
on her bottom.

"Slow down!" puffed Dad.

"I can't run that fast," wailed Peter.

But Horrid Henry raced on.

"Shortcut across the field!" he called.
"Come on slowcoaches!"

The black and white cow grazing alone in the middle raised its head.

"Henry!" shouted Dad. Horrid Henry kept running.

"I don't think that's a cow!"
shouted Mum.

The cow lowered its head
and charged.

"It's a bull!" yelped Mum and Dad.

"RUN!"

Chapter 6

"I said it was dangerous in the countryside!" gasped Henry, as everyone clambered over the stile in the nick of time.

"Look, there's the lake!" he
added, pointing.

Henry ran down to the water's edge.
Peter followed. The embankment
narrowed to a point. Peter slipped
past Henry and bagged the best spot,
right at the water's edge where
the ducks gathered.

"Hey, get away from there,"
said Henry.

"I want to feed the ducks,"
said Peter.

"*I* want to feed the ducks,"
said Henry. "Now move."

"I was here first," said Peter.

"Not any more," said Henry.

Horrid Henry pushed Peter.
"Out of my way, worm!"

Perfect Peter pushed him back.

"Don't call me worm!"

Henry wobbled.

Peter wobbled.

 Splash!

Peter tumbled into the lake.

Crash!

Henry tumbled into the lake.

"My babies!" shrieked Mum,
jumping in after them.

"My – glug glug glug!" shrieked
Dad, jumping into the muddy
water after her.

"My new wellies!" gurgled
Perfect Peter.

Bang!

Pow!

Terminator Gladiator slashed at Rapper Zapper.

Zap!

Rapper Zapper slashed back.

"Go Zappy!" yelled Henry, lying bundled up in blankets on the sofa.

Once everyone had scrambled out of the lake, Mum and Dad had been keen to get home as fast as possible.

"I think the park next time," mumbled Dad, sneezing.

"Definitely," mumbled Mum, coughing.

"Oh, I don't know," said Horrid Henry happily. "A little water never hurt anyone."

What are you going to read next?

Don't miss more mischief with
Horrid Henry . . .

Henry has a very
smelly plan to
defeat Margaret in
**Horrid Henry's
Stinkbomb,**

and battles with
Perfect Peter in
**Horrid Henry
and the Comfy
Black Chair**.

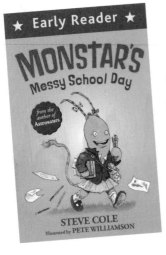

Or for more school stories, discover the magic of **Monstar's Messy School Day**,

and join the Weirdibeasts for fun and games in **Weird Sports Day**.

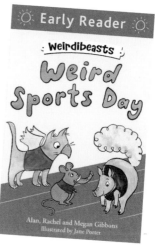

Visit
www.hachettechildrens.co.uk
to discover all the Early Readers